The BIG Violet Book of Beginner Books

The BIG Violet Book of Beginner Books

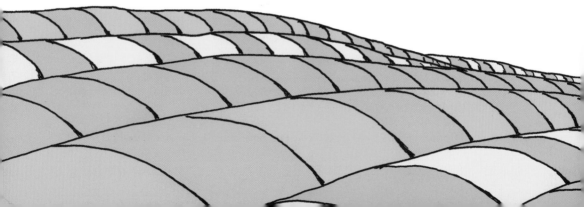

By Dr. Seuss and Alastair Heim

Illustrated by Dr. Seuss,
Tom Brannon, and Katie Kath

Random House 🏠 New York

Contents

The BIG Violet Book of Beginner Books

Dr. Seuss's
BOOK OF
COLORS

You can see yellow.
You can see blue.
You can see other
colors, too.

Green eggs.
Green ham.

Red hat
on Sam-I-am.

Blue turtles.
Gray rock.

Green bird
on pink clock.

Red stripes.
Red tie.
Green book.
Blue sky.

Orange duck.
Blue goo.
Green grass.
Pink shoe.

Brown suit.
Brown hat.

Green umbrella.
Pink mat.

Orange Nink.
Green sink.

Yellow Yink.
Pink drink.

Yellow truck
with purple pots.

Brown beast
with white spots.

Red fox.
Blue socks.

Yellow Knox
in orange box.

Purple fish
in orange tree.
Blue wings
on yellow bee.

Brown camel.
Pink wall.

Red bat.
Blue ball.

Yellow chicks.
Orange blocks.

Brown bricks.
Blue clocks.

Red clothes.
Blue hair.

Gray hat.
Green chair.

Yellow Sneetch.
Green star.

Purple jelly
in a jar.

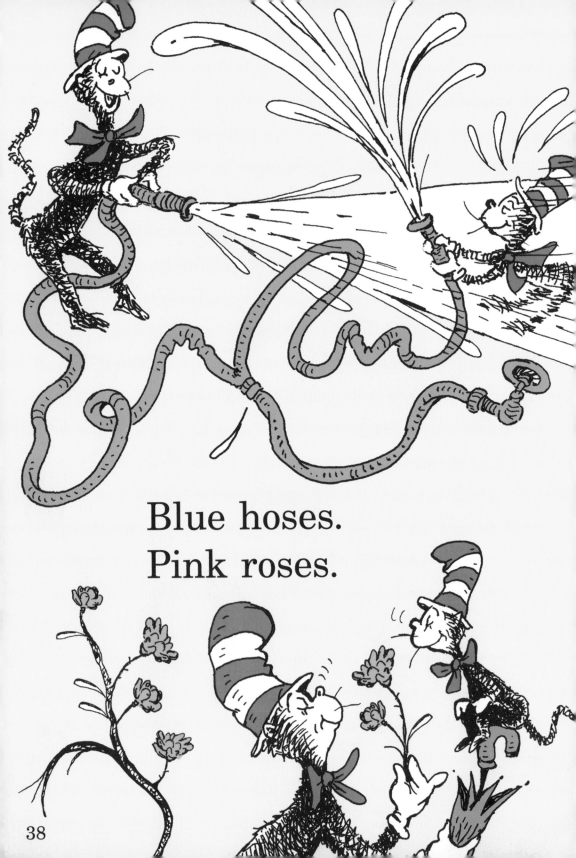

Blue hoses.
Pink roses.

Brown owls
on noses.

Right side up,
or upside down—
Color! Color!
All around!

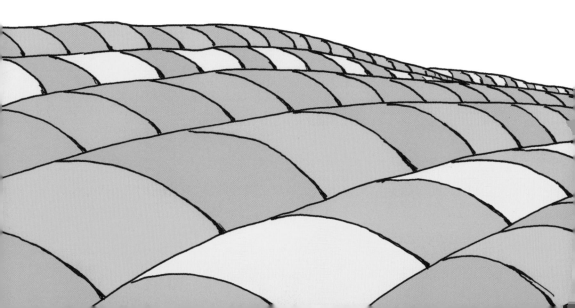

Dr. Seuss's
BOOK OF
ANIMALS

We see animals
all around,
in the sky
and on the ground.

We see a dog.
We see a cat.
We see fish,
thin and fat.

Horse,

cow,

pig,

goat.

Even a crow
in hat and coat.

We see turtles
up in trees.

An animal with two feet.

An animal with four.

An animal with eight feet.

An animal with more!

Some have big teeth.

Some have small.

And some do not
have teeth at all.

This one has feathers.

This one has fuzz.

This one is a
Yuzz-a-ma-Tuzz.

Some animals are shaggy.

Some animals are waggy.

Some are even
ziggy-zaggy!

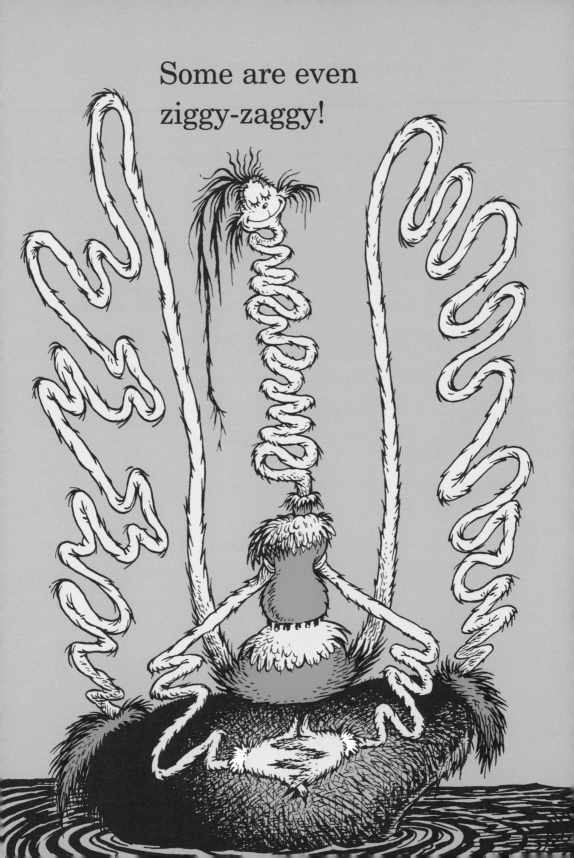

This one has stripes.

This one has spots.

This one has horns.

This one has knots.

Some live inside.

Some live out.

Some like to smile.

Some like to pout.

63

This one works hard.

This one is lazy.

This one's mother
is called Mayzie.

Some sleep in beds.

Some sleep in nests.

Some are called pets.

Some are called pests.

67

Bear and donkey.

Lion and snail.

Mouse and monkey.

Rabbit and whale.

Every day,
from here to there,
animals are
EVERYWHERE!

Dr. Seuss's

1 2 3

1
One

One, one.
It all starts with one.
One cat on a ball
having fun.

2 Two

Two, two.
Next comes two.
Two orange antlers on
Foo-Foo the Snoo.

3 Three

Three, three.
Count to three.
Three birds sitting
in a puffy pink tree.

4 Four

Four, four.
Can you spot four?
Four friends walking
to a big pink door.

5
Five

Five, five.
Do you see five?
Five funny fish
are out for a drive.

6 Six

Look up and down.
Look side to side.
Can you count six
mouths open wide?

7
Seven

This man here
is Mr. Gump.
Mr. Gump has a
seven hump Wump.

8
Eight

Now it's time
to count to eight.
Eight weary elephants
and a tree of great weight.

9
Nine

Nine sad turtles,
each on another's back,
piled up together
in a nine-turtle stack.

10
Ten

Count ten birds.
That's what you should do.
Count ten birds
in yellow and blue.

11
Eleven

Look at his fingers!

One, two, three, four,
five, six, seven,
eight, nine, ten—yikes!
He has eleven!

95

12
Twelve

Can you count twelve
Curious Crandalls?
They sleepwalk on hills
with assorted-sized candles.

98

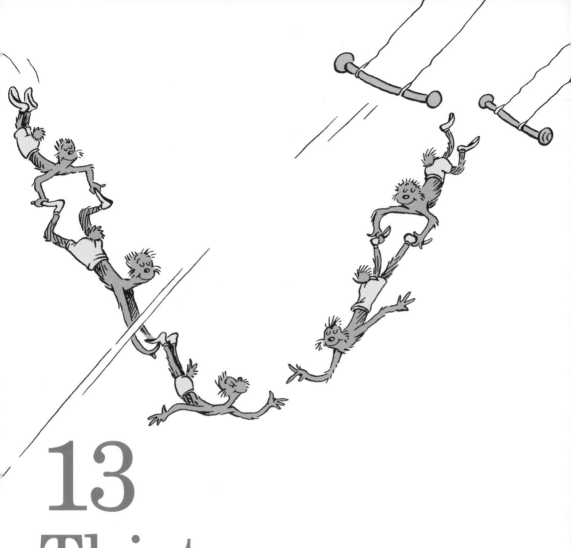

13
Thirteen

Count thirteen trapeezers
of the Zoom-a-Zoop Troupe.
They grab on to each other
as they zoop and they swoop.

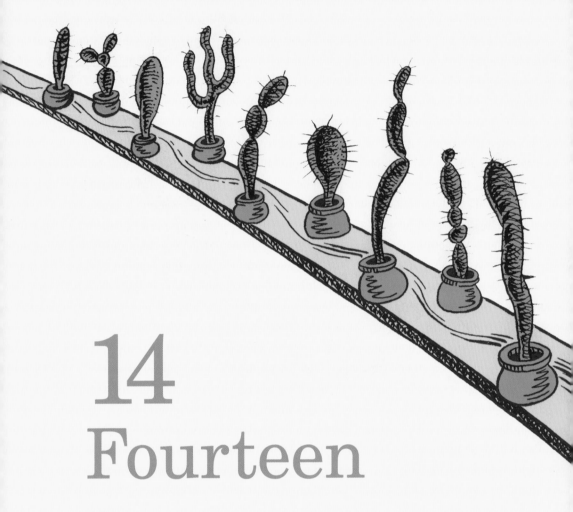

14
Fourteen

Old Mr. Sneelock
on his Roller-Skate-Skis
slides past fourteen pots
full of Stickle-Bush Trees.

15
Fifteen

Count them. Count them.
Count them all.
Fifteen cats sleeping
on a ziggy-zaggy wall.

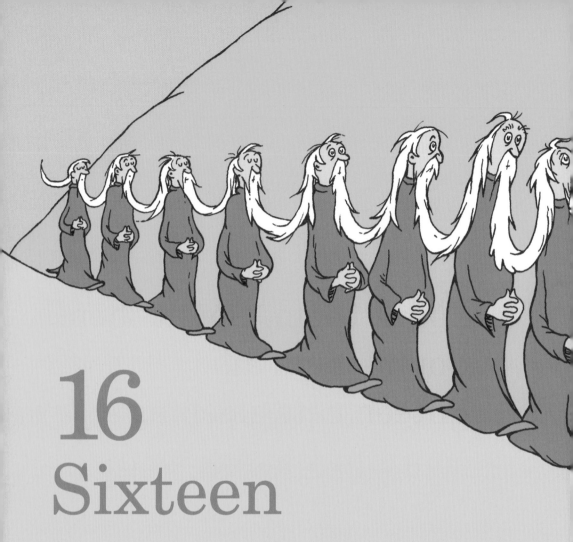

16
Sixteen

Can you count sixteen
of the Brothers Ba-zoo?
They are known far and wide
for the way their hair grew.

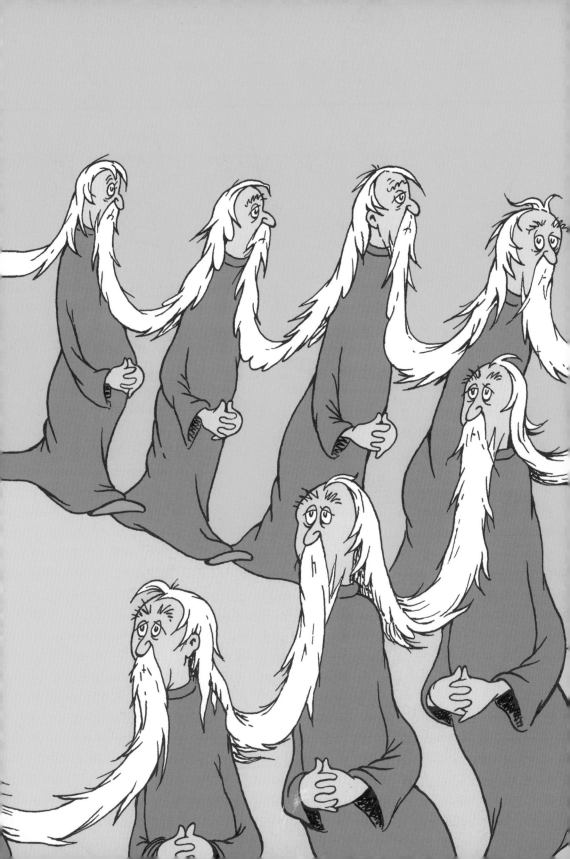

17
Seventeen

And speaking of counting,
you should be quite glad-ish
that you're not this farmer's
seventeenth radish.

18
Eighteen

Count eighteen Jogg-oons
from far desert dunes
who like to croon tunes
about pebbles and prunes.

19
Nineteen

Over the water
and into the sky,
can you count nineteen
bloogs blowing by?

20
Twenty

Start at the bottom.
Work up to the top.
Count twenty Fuddnuddlers.
(And now you can stop.)

COME OVER to MY HOUSE

By Dr. Seuss

Illustrated by Katie Kath

Some houses are bricks

and some houses are sticks.

Some houses are square

and some houses are round.

There are all kinds of houses
around to be found.

Some are on stilts
high up off of the ground.

Some houses are wide.

Some houses
are thin.

Some are so thin
you can hardly get in.

But wherever you go,

you will hear someone say,

"Come over to my house.

Come over and play!"

Come over to my house.

The fishing is great!

They bite all the time

and you don't have to wait.

Come over some day

and bring plenty of bait.

My house has a kite
that can whistle and sing!
Come over some day
and bring plenty of string.

My house has so many
big pine trees outside,
we can slide on my
wonderful pine needle slide.

The roof of my house
has a stork on a nest.

The roof of my house
is a good place to rest.

You can play on my roof.
But my house is so tall,
it's a long way downstairs
to go after the ball.

My house is bright pink
and it's happy and gay.
Our streets are wet water.
We like it that way.

Come up on my porch
and I'll give you a treat.
Spaghetti!
We'll eat
and we'll eat and we'll eat.
We'll eat twenty miles of it!
We'll eat a ton!
Food, at my house,
is such wonderful fun.

Come over to my house
and sit by the fire.

My fire burns trees
and it's hotter and higher.

Our fire's in a stove.
It makes beautiful heat.
Come over! Come over
and warm your cold feet.

Come over to my house.

I live on a boat.

I live in a city

of houses that float.

Come into my houseboat.
Have supper with me.
I'll give you cold rice
and a cup of hot tea.

I eat with chopsticks
and you can learn how.
But, boy, you are
terribly sloppy right now.

137

Come over to my house
and stay for the night.
We have 200 rooms,
so I'm sure it's all right.
But don't touch the tigers.
They're liable to bite.

In my house, my bath
is a fancy machine
with handles and spouts
and it's long and it's green.

I just have a tub
but I keep just as clean.

At our house, hot water comes out of the rocks. It's handy for washing ourselves and our socks.

Come over to our house.
You'll like our bath, too.
Especially if you have
some laundry to do.

Over at my house
you'll eat funny fruit.
You'll ride on my llama
and toot on my flute.

My house has books!
And they're all very fine.
I'll learn to read yours
if you'll learn to read mine.

In a faraway place,
in a wide empty land,
my house is a tent
in the wind and the sand.

At my house I'll show you
a wonderful show

in the night in the sky

when the Northern Lights glow.

My house has an ostrich.

Hop on! Take a ride.

But watch where you're riding!

Don't ride him inside!

In back of my house
lives a red kangaroo,
two koala bears,
and an emu or two.
Come over and play.
We're all waiting for you!

My house is quite cold.

I need fur to sleep in.

My house is quite hot.

I just sleep in my skin.

I sleep in a bed
with a big puffy puff.
Come over some night,
we have puff puffs enough.

In my house I sleep
on a mat on the floor.
There's a mat here for you.
But I hope you don't snore.

Come over to my house
and we'll milk a cow.
It isn't too hard
and it's time you learned how.

You can milk goats
at my house,
so come with your pail.
It's easy.
You'll find the milk
back near the tail.

159

My house has a reindeer.
Come on! Don't be shy.
Step up and start milking.
Let's give it a try.

Every house in the world
has a ceiling and floor.
But the ones you'll like best
have a wide-open door.

Some houses are rich,
full of silver and gold.

And some are quite poor,
sort of empty and old.

Some houses are marble

and some are just tin.

But they're all,
all alike
when a friend
asks you in.

There are so many houses
you'll meet on your way.
And wherever you go,
you will hear someone say . . .

"Come over to my house!
Come over and play."

WHAT PET SHOULD I GET?
By Dr. Seuss

We want a pet.
We want a pet.
What kind of pet
should we get?

Dad said we could have one.

Dad said he would pay.

I went to the Pet Shop.

I went there with Kay.

And so we went in . . .

I took one fast look . . .

I saw a fine dog who shook hands.

So we shook.

So I said,

"I want him!"

But then, Kay saw a cat.

She gave it a pat,

and she said, "I want THAT!"

Then Kay said, "Now what

do you think we should do?

Dad said to pick one.

We can not take home two."

Then what do you know?
We saw two other kinds.
NOW how could Kay and I
make up our minds?

A pup and a kitten.

They looked like good fun.

NOW which would we pick?

We could only pick one.

The cat?

Or the dog?

The kitten?

The pup?

Oh, boy!
It is something
to make a mind up.

Then I looked all around.
I saw something with wings.
I said, "Look at him!
We can pick one that sings."

But THEN ...

"Look over there!"
said my sister Kay.
"We can go home
with a rabbit today!"

Then I looked at Kay.

I said, "What will we do?

I like all the pets that I see.

So do you.

We have to pick ONE pet
and pick it out soon.
You know Mother told us
to be back by noon."

And I could have done it.
I could have, I bet.
I could have said
what pet we should get.

BUT . . .

you know what Kay did . . .

Do you know what she did?

She said, "FISH!

     FISH!

       FISH!

       FISH!

It may be a fish

is the pet that we wish!"

THEN . . .

I saw a new kind!

And they were good, too!

How could I pick one?

Now what should we do?

We could only pick one.

That is what my dad said.

But how could I make up

that mind in my head?

Pick a pet fast!
Pick one out soon!

Mother and Dad said
to be home by noon!

The time may be now
to make up my mind.
But who knows what other
good pets I might find?

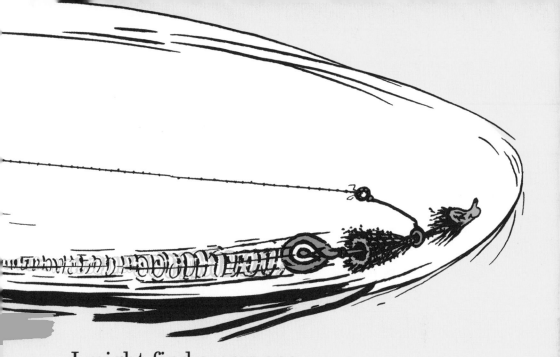

I might find a new one.

A fast kind of thing

who would fly round my head

in a ring on a string!

Yes, that would be fun . . .

BUT . . .

our house is so small.

This thing on a string

would bump, bump into the wall!

My mother, I know,

would not like that at all.

SO, maybe some other
good kind of pet.
Another kind maybe
is what we should get.

We might find a new kind.
A pet who is tall.
A tall pet who fits
in a space that is small.

My mother might like
this pet best of them all.

If we had a big tent,
then we would be able
to take home a YENT!
Dad would like us
to have a good YENT.
BUT, how do I know
he would pay for a tent?

So, you see how it is
when you pick out a pet.
How can you make up
your mind what to get?

BUT . . .

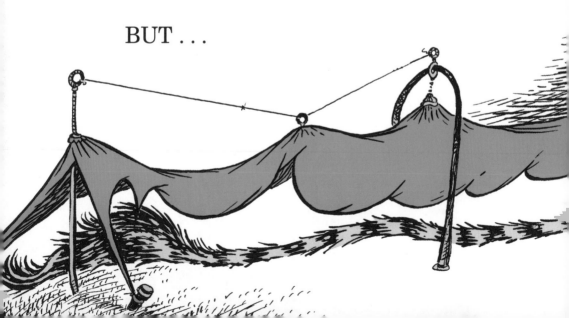

What if we took
one of each kind of pet?
Then our house would be full
of the pets we would get.

NO . . .

Dad would be mad.

We can only have one.

If we do not choose,

we will end up with NONE.

"I will do it right now.
I will do it!" I said.
"I will make up the mind
that is up in my head."

The dog . . . ? Or the rabbit . . . ?
The fish . . . ? Or the cat . . . ?
I picked one out fast,
and then that was that.

203

IF I RAN YOUR SCHOOL

by **the Cat in the Hat**
with a little help from **Alastair Heim**

illustrated by **Tom Brannon**

I just heard a thing
so I came right away!
The KING of all unfunny
things, I must say . . .

I heard that you two—
or, perhaps, maybe YOU—
think going to school
is a DULL thing to do.
I came here to show you
that school can be FUN!
I showed up to show you
how school fun is DONE.

If I ran your school,
we would start every day
in a PLEDGE-FULLY way
as we stand up and say . . .

"Today I will learn
how much fun FUN can be!
From eight after eight
until three after three,
I will smile all the while
with a grin on my chin
till the end of the day
from the time we begin!"

If I ran your school,
we would get a class pet.
But not just ONE pet . . .
ALL the pets we can get!

Some would be FUZZY
and some would be WET,
and others would come
as a TWO-FOR-ONE set.

If I ran your school,
I would help you to read
by giving each student
a BOOK-BLOOMING SEED.

Each seed would be planted
and grown in a pot.
And after we water
and water A LOT . . .

. . . the seeds would sprout BOOKS
that would fill up the room!
The more that you read them,
the more YOU would bloom!

2 + 3 = 5

If I ran your school,
I would give a POP QUIZ
where we take and we shake
every bottle there is
until they EXPLODE
into fountains of FIZZ.

2 + 2 = 4

1 + 2 = 3

2 + 3 = 6

And IF you can guess
how much FIZZ that there is,
it TRULY would make you
a POP FIZZ QUIZ WHIZ!

If I ran your school,
on the days you have art,
I would drive all around
in my ART-MAKING CART.

My CART-TO-MAKE-ART
would have glitter and glue
and LOTS of fun things
that are perfect for you.

At twelve after twelve,
we would serve a buffet
of pizzas and pancakes
and tray after tray
of berries and cherries
and swirly sorbet
to keep you well fed
for the rest of the day.

If I ran your school,
we would cover your sneakers
in DOUBLE-BOUNCE BUBBLES
we brew in these beakers
to give your old sneakers
a little more pep . . .

. . . and put a new SCIENCE-Y
spring in your step!

If I ran your school,
we would play a FUN song.
While I waved this wood wand
and you all played along . . .

The DRUMMERS and FLUTERS
and TUBA TOOT-TOOTERS,
and ALL of the players
with sliding trombones
and THREE-NOZZLED BLOOZERS
and SAX-A-MA-PHONES,
would take their tune makers
and turn them around
and play them all BACKWARD.
Just THINK of the sound!

If I ran your school,
we would have SMELL-AND-TELL,
where you bring in a thing
(and that thing has a smell).

We would smell that thing well
as you stand up and tell
how the thing that you bring
got its good or bad smell.

If I ran your school,
I would sit in the bleachers
and cheer you all on,
right along with your teachers,
through round after round
after round after round
of SCHOOL-A-HOOP HOOPLA
to see who gets crowned . . .

. . . as the HOOPLA-HOOP Queen
and the HOOPLA-HOOP King.
The new Queen and King
of all SCHOOL-A-HOOPING!

If I ran your school,
at your very last class,
you ALL would be getting
a GO WILD PASS!

Your classes are over!
Your school day is done!
And NOW it is time
for some fun in the sun!

Then ALL of my Little Cat
crew would be there
to welcome you all
to their LITTLE CAT FAIR!
The games and the rides
and the LOOP-THE-LOOP slides
and the EXTRA-fun prizes
that come in all sizes
should keep you all smiling
the whole school year through . . .

If I ran your school,
THAT is what I would do,
then tip my top hat and say
"FAIR-WELL" to you!
There MAY be more schools
that will need me, you see,
to show them how FUN
that THEIR school day can be . . .

Do YOU think your school
needs a visit from me?

Dr. Seuss

THEODOR SEUSS GEISEL—aka Dr. Seuss—is one of the most beloved children's book authors of all time. From *The Cat in the Hat* to *Oh, the Places You'll Go!*, his iconic characters, stories, and art style have had a lasting influence on generations of children and adults. The books he wrote and illustrated under the name Dr. Seuss (and others he wrote, but did not illustrate, under the pseudonyms Theo. LeSieg and Rosetta Stone) have been translated into fifty languages. Hundreds of millions of copies have found their way into homes around the world. Dr. Seuss's long list of awards includes Caldecott Honors, the Pulitzer Prize, and eight honorary doctorates. Works based on his original stories have won three Oscars, three Emmys, three Grammys, and a Peabody.